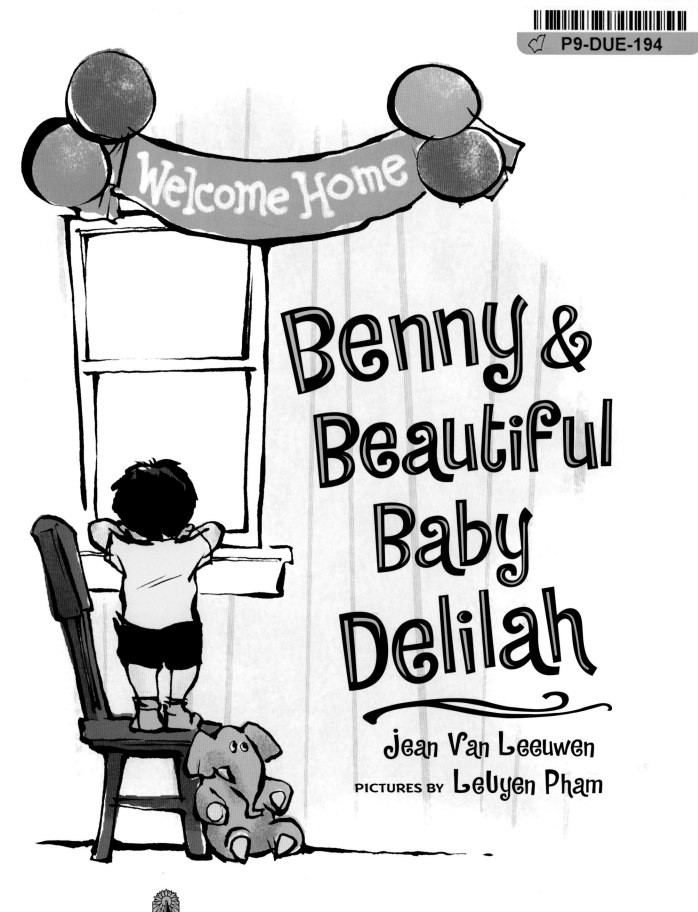

Welcome Home

Benny & Beautiful Baby Delilah

Jean Van Leeuwen

PICTURES BY LeUyen Pham

DIAL BOOKS FOR YOUNG READERS

To my older brother, Hung, for all of his big-brotherly ways . . .
—L.P.

DIAL BOOKS FOR YOUNG READERS
A division of Penguin Young Readers Group
Published by The Penguin Group • Penguin Group (USA) Inc., 375 Hudson
Street, New York, NY 10014, U.S.A. • Penguin Group (Canada), 90 Eglinton
Avenue East, Suite 700, Toronto, Ontario, Canada M4P 2Y3 (a division of
Pearson Penguin Canada Inc.) • Penguin Books Ltd, 80 Strand, London WC2R
0RL, England • Penguin Ireland, 25 St. Stephen's Green, Dublin 2, Ireland
(a division of Penguin Books Ltd) • Penguin Group (Australia), 250
Camberwell Road, Camberwell, Victoria 3124, Australia (a division of Pearson
Australia Group Pty Ltd) • Penguin Books India Pvt Ltd, 11 Community
Centre, Panchsheel Park, New Delhi-110 017, India • Penguin Group (NZ), Cnr
Airborne and Rosedale Roads, Albany, Auckland 1310, New Zealand (a division
of Pearson New Zealand Ltd) • Penguin Books (South Africa)
(Pty) Ltd, 24 Sturdee Avenue, Rosebank, Johannesburg 2196,
South Africa • Penguin Books Ltd, Registered Offices:
80 Strand, London WC2R 0RL, England

Designed by Teresa Kietlinski
Text set in Clarendon
Manufactured in China on acid-free paper

10 9 8 7 6 5 4 3 2 1

Library of Congress Cataloging-in-Publication Data
Van Leeuwen, Jean.
Benny and beautiful baby Delilah /
Jean Van Leeuwen ; pictures by LeUyen Pham.
    p.   cm.
Summary: Benny is not pleased when his new baby
sister, Delilah, arrives at his house.
ISBN 0-8037-2891-3
[1. Babies—Fiction. 2. Brothers and sisters—Fiction.]
I. Pham, LeUyen, ill. II. Title.
PZ7.V3273Bh 2006   [E]—dc22   2004019412

Children's Room

One day a baby came to stay at Benny's house.
Her name was Delilah.

"Isn't she **beautiful**?" said Dad.
        Benny wasn't so sure.
Beautiful was a red fire truck.
        Beautiful was a Tyrannosaurus rex.

"She is your very own little sister," said Mom.
        "You can hold her and play with her
and help take care of her."

But when Benny held Baby Delilah, she cried.

She was **too little** to play trucks.

But she was **too big** too.

She took up lots of room with all her
baby toys and baby noise.

She took Benny's bed.

"That was your baby bed," said Dad.
"You have a big-boy bed now."

She took Benny's place
on Mom's lap.

Dad's was good too,
of course,
but not so cozy soft.

And she took Benny's time.

His story time.

His tickle time.

His shaving-with-Dad
time.

At night in his big-boy bed,
Benny whispered in his elephant's ear.

"She's **not** beautiful.
I don't even **like her**."

Everyone came to see Baby Delilah.
Grandmas and grandpas, aunts and uncles,
and a zillion cousins.

"Will you look at those big brown eyes!" said Grandma.
"I can count," said Benny. "Want to hear me?
One, two, forty-leven."

Only no one was listening.
"Why, she's the spitting image of
Great-Aunt Pearl!" said Uncle Arthur.

"I can do a tumblesault," said Benny.

He did a **perfect** tumblesault.

Only he landed on the silly twins, who **always** cried.

"Isn't she precious?
I could just eat her up!" said Aunt Sophie.

Good idea, thought Benny.

"I can run," he said, "and I can jump and I can even fly."

He ran around and jumped
on the sofa and flew
down the stairs.
Only he knocked over a few things.

Dad caught him.
"Say good night, big guy," he said.
And he flew Benny
all the way to his bed.

"It's not **fair**," Benny grumbled into his elephant's ear.
"I have to go to bed
before a **baby**."

Baby Delilah
was **not**
beautiful.

"She has no hair and no teeth," said Benny.
"She looks like a chipmunk and
she cries all the time."

"That's true," Mom agreed.

"Couldn't we take her back and get
a new, quieter one?" asked Benny.

"No, we couldn't," said Dad.
"Baby Delilah is here to stay."

When Mom and Dad weren't looking,
Benny sang her a song.

I don't like you, Delilah.
You can't even smile.
You're a teeny tiny
Weeny whiny
Crying little baby.

Baby Delilah didn't like his song.
She cried even more.

She cried in the morning.

She cried at night.

She cried in the middle
of the night.

No one could sleep.
"I told you," said Benny.

Mom held Baby Delilah and rocked her and sang her
lullabies. Dad walked her all around the house.
But Baby Delilah kept crying.
She sounded like a fire truck.

"What are we going to do?" asked Mom.
Benny had an idea.

"I can do a magic trick," he said.
He waved his magic wand.

"Poof! I'm a monkey."
Benny jumped around and
chitter-chattered and ate bananas.
But Baby Delilah kept crying.

"Hey, Baby Delilah!" said Benny. "Watch this."

He hung upside
down by his tail.

But Baby Delilah
kept crying.

"Okay," said Benny. "How about this?"
He made his worst monkey face.

Baby Delilah looked at him.

"Glug," she said. And she smiled.

It was like **the sun** coming out.

"Well, would you look at that," said Dad.

"Her first smile," said Mom.

She *is* beautiful, thought Benny.

His very own little sister.

Beautiful Baby Delilah.